This book belongs to

. . . .

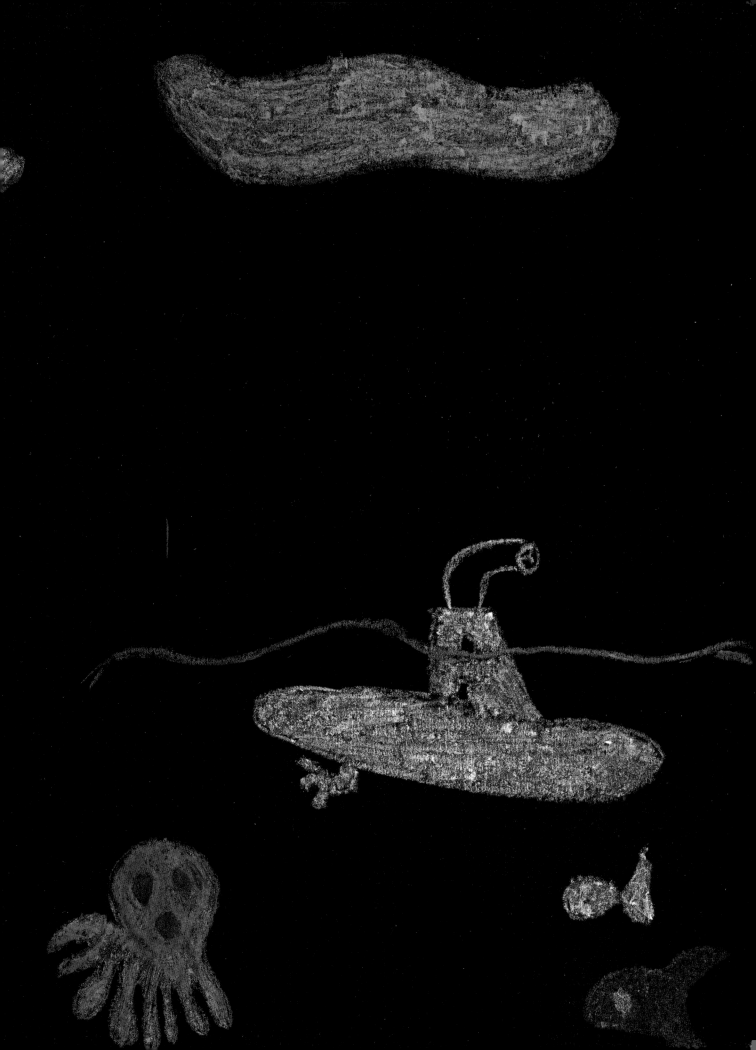

Front endpapers by Ricardo Jorge Pereira da Silva aged 8
Back endpapers by Sara Nogueira Soares aged 9
Thank you to José Jorge Letria Primary School, Cascais, Portugal,
Cascais Public Library at Casa da Horta da Quinta de Santa Clara
and Cascais Town Council for all their help with the endpapers K.P.

For Pat, who loves the sea V.T.
For Harriet Bayly and her family K.P.

OXFORD
UNIVERSITY PRESS

Great Clarendon Street, Oxford OX2 6DP

Oxford University Press is a department of the University of Oxford.
It furthers the University's objective of excellence in research, scholarship,
and education by publishing worldwide in

Oxford New York

Auckland Cape Town Dar es Salaam Hong Kong Karachi
Kuala Lumpur Madrid Melbourne Mexico City Nairobi
New Delhi Shanghai Taipei Toronto

With offices in
Argentina Austria Brazil Chile Czech Republic France Greece
Guatemala Hungary Italy Japan Poland Portugal Singapore
South Korea Switzerland Thailand Turkey Ukraine Vietnam

© Text copyright Valerie Thomas 2011
© Illustrations copyright Korky Paul 2011
The moral rights of the author and artist have been asserted

Database right Oxford University Press (maker)

First published 2011

British Library Cataloguing in Publication Data available

ISBN: 978-0-19-275747-0 (hardback)
ISBN: 978-0-19-275748-7 (paperback)
ISBN: 978-0-19-275749-4 (paperback with audio CD)

2 4 6 8 10 9 7 5 3 1

Printed in Singapore

Paper used in the production of this book is a natural, recyclable product made
from wood grown in sustainable forests. The manufacturing process conforms
to the environmental regulations of the country of origin

Valerie Thomas and Korky Paul

Winnie
Under the Sea

OXFORD
UNIVERSITY PRESS

It was holiday time for Winnie the Witch and her big black cat, Wilbur.

'Where will we go this year, Wilbur?' asked Winnie. She searched the internet and found a little island, with blue sea, golden sand, and coconut trees.

The bright blue sea was full of beautiful fish.
'Don't the fish look lovely, Wilbur?' she said.
'They look delicious,' thought Wilbur.
'That's where we'll go,' said Winnie.

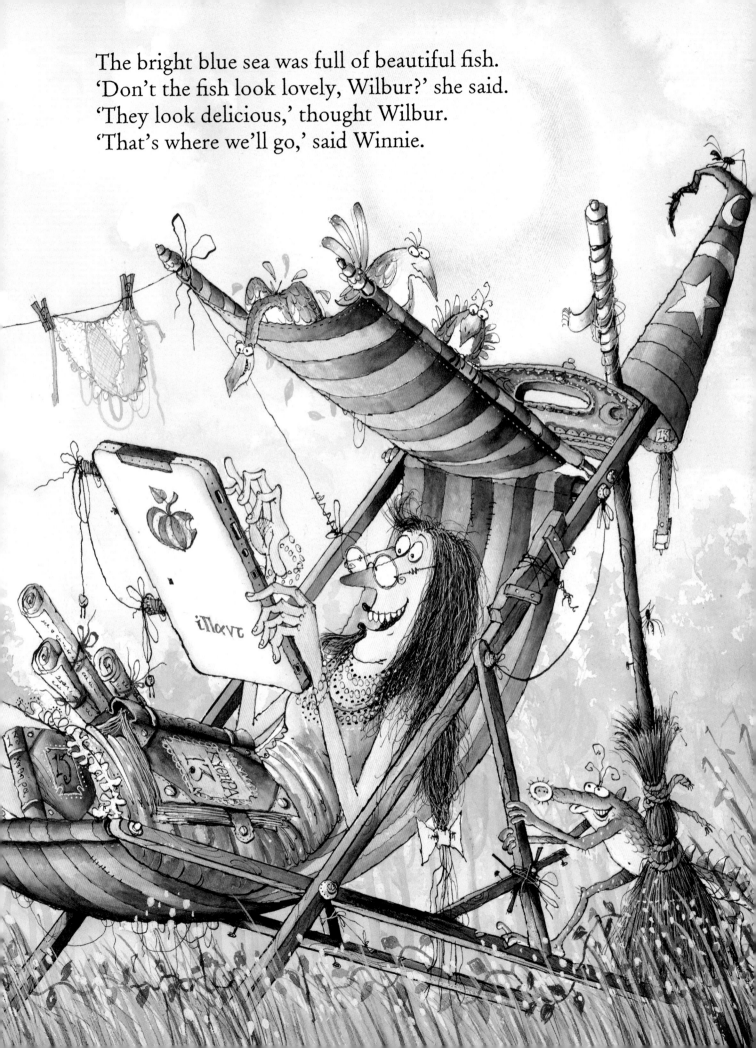

She packed her suitcase,
Wilbur jumped onto her shoulder,
and they zoomed up into the sky.

At last, there was the island.
It did look lovely.

They landed on the golden sand,
and found a comfortable hut.

Winnie put on her flippers and her goggles,
and dived into the water.

Wilbur climbed a coconut tree.
That was fun.
Then he had a sleep.
That was peaceful.

Winnie was having a lovely time.
The sea was full of fish.
There were dolphins,
turtles, and coral.
It was so beautiful.
Winnie wanted Wilbur
to see it, too.

'Wilbur,' called Winnie,
'come and see the fish.
You'll love them!'

Wilbur wanted to see the fish.
He put one paw in the water.
Erk! Nasty! It was wet!
'Meeeeoooow!' cried Wilbur.
He hated getting wet.

Then Winnie had
a wonderful idea.
She waved her
magic wand, shouted,

Abracadabra!

and Wilbur was
no longer a cat.

He was a cat-fish!

Wilbur the cat-fish dived
into the waves and swam away.

Winnie watched him through her goggles.

He chased some tiny fish.
Then he dived under a dogfish
and played catch with a crayfish.

Wilbur the cat-fish was having so much fun,
Winnie wanted to be a fish as well.

But she couldn't be a fish.
She had to hold her magic wand.
What could she be?
Of course!

Winnie waved her wand, shouted,

Abracadabra!

and she was an octopus!
An octopus with orange
and yellow legs, holding
a magic wand!

It was fun being an octopus.
Winnie the octopus waved her eight legs
and floated through the seaweed,
around the coral, over the rocks.

Wilbur the cat-fish darted around her.
Thousands of fish swam with them.
Tiny fish, big fish, and, suddenly . . .

a sea lion.

The sea lion flipped its tail, and Winnie lost her wand.

She grabbed at it, but missed.

A swordfish tried to spear it for her, but missed.

A jellyfish nearly caught it, but missed.

Down, down it sank,

into the wreck of
an old sailing ship,

and disappeared.

'Blithering broomsticks!' wailed Winnie,
but it sounded like, 'Bubble, bubble, bubble.'
'Bubble, bubble, bubble,' cried Wilbur.

They didn't want to stay under the sea for ever.
Where was the magic wand?
Stuck in the anchor? *No.*

Under the ropes? *No.*   Behind the big crab? *No.*

Wilbur flipped it out.
Winnie grabbed it,
waved it five times,
shouted,

Abracadabra!

In the treasure chest? **Yes!**

and a **witch** and a **cat** floated back to the shore.

'That was exciting, Wilbur,' Winnie said.
'Too exciting. We won't do that again.
But it is beautiful under the sea.'

Then Winnie had another wonderful idea.

A little yellow boat was bobbing on the waves.
Winnie waved her magic wand, shouted,

GHOTI

Abracadabra!

and there, bobbing on the waves . . .

was a yellow submarine.

Winnie and Wilbur went on board.
The fish swam up to the windows and looked in.

'It is lovely under the sea, isn't it Wilbur,' said Winnie.
'It's lovely and dry in here,' Wilbur thought.
'Purr, purr, purr,' he said.

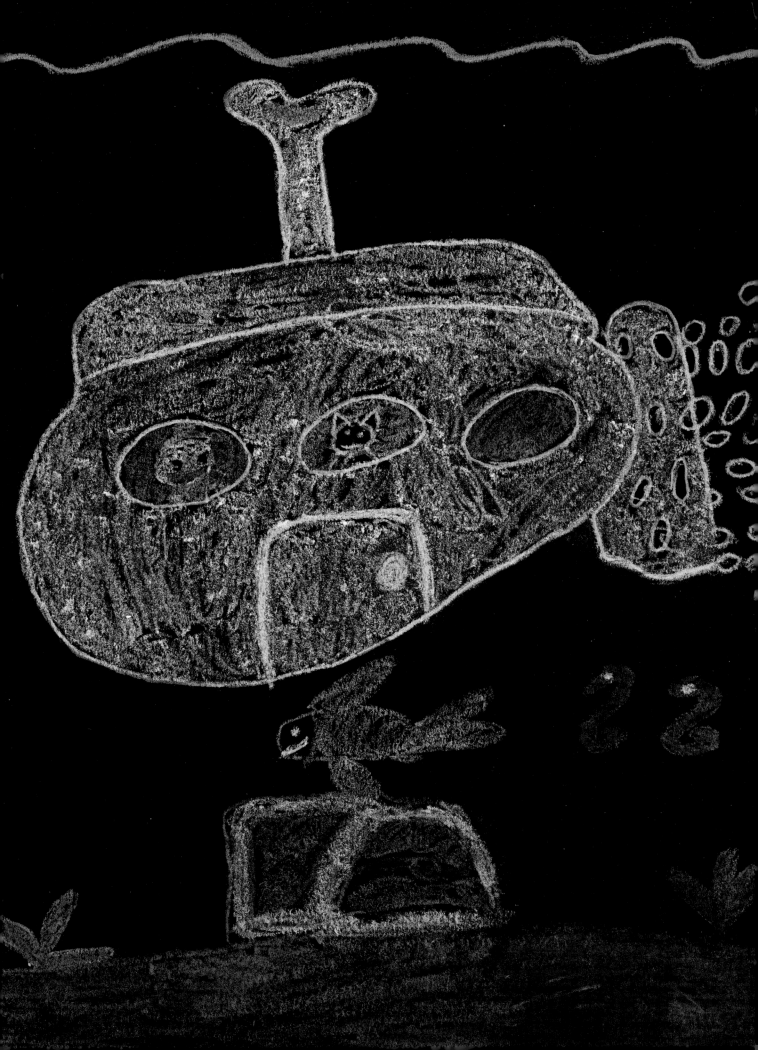

Winnie's Under the Sea Biscuits

Ingredients

150G OR 1 CUP BUTTER

75G OR 1/2 CUP CASTER SUGAR

225G OR 2 CUPS PLAIN FLOUR

HALF A TEASPOON OF VANILLA EXTRACT

ICING SUGAR, FOOD COLOURING, SPRINKLES AND SILVER BALLS TO DECORATE

A LARGE LIGHTLY GREASED BAKING SHEET

LARGE AND SMALL HEART-SHAPED COOKIE CUTTERS AND A STAR-SHAPED COOKIE CUTTER

Method

Preheat the oven to 170°C / 375F or gas mark 5

Cut the butter into cubes and place in a bowl. Add the sugar, flour, and vanilla extract. Rub all the ingredients together until you have a smooth dough. Shape the dough into a ball, wrap it in cling film and place in the fridge for 10 minutes. Roll the dough out on a floured surface. It needs to be half a centimetre thick.

Cutting the biscuits

Use the star-shaped cutter to make starfish biscuits. To make fish biscuits cut a large and a small heart shape from the dough. For each fish, place two heart shapes together on the baking sheet so that the point of the smaller heart fits into the 'v' of the larger heart. The mixture will bake together, forming one fish-shaped biscuit.

Baking and decorating

Bake in the oven for 15-20 minutes until the biscuits are a light golden colour. Leave them to cool completely on a wire rack. Mix together some icing sugar, food colouring and a little warm water. Using an icing bag with nozzle, drizzle icing on top of your biscuits and decorate with sprinkles and silver balls.

Leave to set and enjoy!